The Little Engineer
A Christmas Short Story

(Based on The Little Engine
That Could)

By A.J. Warkowski

Dorrance Publishing Co
585 Alpha Drive
Pittsburgh, PA 15238
Visit our website at www.dorrancebookstore.com

ISBN: 979-8-89341-469-1
eISBN: 979-8-89341-968-9

For Raylan & Sawyer

In memory of Paul O'Neill, whose Christmas
spirit and storytelling helped inspire this.

It was Christmas Eve so Connie was at the Garrison railway depot early. She couldn't wait to get the Christmas train rolling. For 50 years now the Christmas train delivered Christmas presents and food to the six towns over the Cheyenne Pass in the mountains. The tradition started before the roads into the mountains were developed to bring presents and meals for Christmas to the hard to reach and poor mountain towns. It had been running before even her parents were born. She remembered it coming to town each Christmas Eve as a little girl growing up in the town of O'Neill. It was the last stop on the train's run. The annual event was the biggest reason she had developed a love for trains and now she was finally going to drive it herself. For the past four years she had gone with Hank on the Christmas run. Now, as the depot manager, he was confident Connie could run the train on her own and had signed off on her engineer license. She had been working on the tour train in the valley and local freight runs for almost five years, knew the route through the Cheyenne Pass like the back of her hand, and every detail of old engine #24 by heart. She was ready to take over the Christmas train.

In the years since the Christmas train started, the roads into the mountains had greatly improved, access by truck became practical, and the people who lived up there were much better off. However, the Christmas train had become a tradition that everyone in the mountains enjoyed and looked forward to every holiday season. Through the rest of the year, engine #24 pulled a tour train. On Christmas Eve, it was dedicated to the Christmas trip into the mountains. In the weeks leading up to Christmas, donations were collected in the city of Garrison and the surrounding areas, then loaded into twelve cars, one car of presents and one car of meals for each town. All the cars were dressed up in red and green.

Connie trotted past the museum piece in front of the Garrison Depot. It was engine #307 known as Old Ben. She greeted everyone she passed with an enthusiastic "Merry Christmas!" waving with one arm as she cradled a box for the Christmas train under the other. Old Ben was decorated for the season too, with Christmas lights, garland, and a big wreath on the front so the number 307 was right in the middle.

"Merry Christmas, Hank!" Connie shouted as she approached the depot manager.

"Merry Christmas, Connie," he turned and replied with a chuckle in his southern drawl.

"I suppose I don't have to ask if you're ready for your run."

"No, you don't," her big doe eyes beaming, "I've been ready my whole life." Hank was a good friend of Connie's father, had watched her grow up, and was happy to help her get into railroading. He knew what today meant for her.

"Have you seen the Nativity up in O'Neill yet?" he asked.

"No, I haven't been up there yet this season," as she paused for a moment, "but I saw them at Franklin's when he finished carving them before Thanksgiving." The town of O'Neill had ordered a new life size Nativity set from Franklin's wood shop in Garrison.

"I can't wait to see them in the town square," she said as she resumed her pace, practically skipping as she entered the loading dock area where Louis, the dock supervisor, was.

"Merry Christmas, Louis!" she greeted.

"Merry Christmas, Connie," the big, tall man bellowed in his deep voice with a grin as wide as one of arms was around. He was the type who was no stranger to physical labor. "We're just loading some last minute donations. It'll be ready in about half an hour." The six foot plus Louis dwarfed the five foot tall Connie.

"Great! What's the total weight?" she asked.

"Gonna come to just over 500 tons with your tender," he informed her.

"Not as much as the old days," she reflected. Years ago, the Christmas runs were full loads. These days, there were as many presents from people who simply had family and friends in the mountains and used the tradition of the train to send them their gifts. Some parents who lived in the mountains would actually come into Garrison to drop off presents for their children just so it could be delivered by the train. Kids loved to get a present or two off the Christmas train. It was like a second Santa, only where they never saw Santa, they got to see engine 24 pull in with their presents.

"It's not a bad thing. Less people in need these days," posed Louis.

"Well, even if there was one present on board, I'd drive it up there. Heck, even if it was nothing but pure Christmas cheer, I'd haul it," Connie proclaimed enthusiastically.

"I know you would," Louis said with a slight laugh.

"Oh, would you put this in car 1?" she asked and handed Louis the box she had been carrying.

"Sure thing, Connie."

Every package on the train was addressed to a specific person or family. Those who were in need, would apply earlier in the season and packages were made especially for them.

"I'll get #24, pull 'er around, and hook up."

"I think Charlie is getting the boiler warmed up for you now," Louis informed her.

"Oh, he didn't have to do that," she said as she jumped onto the back of one of the cars to cross the tracks on her way to the roundhouse.

When she got there, sure enough, there was Charlie, waiting for Connie. Charlie was the last mechanic who had started out working on steam engines, like #24. He could fix up the new diesels as good as anyone but no one took care of the old steamers like Charlie. Engine 24 was a 4-8-0 type steam locomotive, two leading axles and four drive axles. A medium size locomotive as steamers went. Nothing like the old big boys or a modern diesel engine but it had what it took to pull the little Christmas train into the mountains.

"Merry Christmas, Miss Connie," the old engine mechanic greeted her as she entered the roundhouse. He was standing next to the engine with his hands tucked into the front of his overalls.

"Merry Christmas, Charlie!" she came back, "and congratulations.   You're the first person today to beat me to saying 'Merry Christmas'."

"Do I win a prize?" he asked sarcastically.

"Uh…" Connie thought for a moment, "buy you coffee at Dela's Café."

"You know my wife gives me her coffee for free."   Charlie and Dela had been married for over 40 years.

"I'll think of something," she said.   "I guess I owe you double for getting 24 started. You know you didn't have to do that for me."

"I know it's your big day. I wanted to do it."

"I appreciate it," she called over her shoulder as she climbed up into the engine cab.

"All right Miss Connie, I'll get on the turntable and spin you around," Charlie said and walked over to the turntable's doghouse. Working the controls, he lined up the turntable with the bay that engine 24 occupied.

The Johnson bar controlled the direction of the engine and how long steam was injected into the cylinders.   She moved it forward, eased the throttle open, and #24 chugged slowly onto the turntable.   As the engine and tender neared the center, she cut the pressure, put the Johnson bar in neutral, and pulled the brake, stopping on the turntable so the engine and tender were balanced.   No sooner did it come to a halt, she gave Charlie a thumbs up and he had the turntable rotating. When the turntable track was lined up with the main track, he stopped it, locked the turntable with the main line, and gave Connie a thumbs up of his own.

Engine 24 rolled up passed the switch junction and stopped. When she saw the signal that the switchman had moved the track switch to the loading dock line, Connie put the Johnson bar into reverse and backed up to the waiting twelve cars.   The porters were closing up the doors on the boxcars. As each one shut, Louis was making final checks on his clipboard. When he got to the first car, he waved Connie on as she backed up the locomotive. #24 eased into the first car; with a clank and slight jolt, the engine and tender were coupled. Connie jumped out, jogged around the coal tender to the first car, and Louis helped her connect the brake lines.

"Looks like you're all set," Louis stated when they were done.

"I'll check in with Alice and grab a hot coco to go while the automatic brakes charge," she bubbled. The automatic brakes controlled the cars and took a minute for the air to fill the lines all the way back.

Connie was truly a kid at heart when it came to Christmas and trains. Who said the magic of the holiday had to fade when you grew up?

"Merry Christmas, Alice," Connie greeted as she walked up to the dispatch counter. As dispatcher, Alice tracked all the trains. "How're we looking?"

"Merry Christmas, Connie Dear," the blonde, middle aged dispatcher greeted as she stood shuffling some files in a cabinet. She rolled the drawer she was working in shut, then turned and looked down through the counter window at Connie. "The North-Union just cleared Cheyenne Pass with some miners and equipment." Sitting down in her wheelie chair and turning to her big schedule board behind her, Alice continued, "No one else going through for at least another 36 hours so you're all clear, kiddo."

"Thanks. What about the weather?" Connie asked.

"Clear skies into late afternoon," Alice said as she spun back around. Sitting in her chair, she was now eye to eye with the little engineer. "50% chance of snow in the mountains starting in the early evening with the usual early winter temperatures.   Nothing to worry about, hon.”

“A little snow during Santa’s night is appropriate,” Connie noted.

“And a good snow pack is always needed.   It started building early this season so the reservoirs should be in good shape come spring,” Alice added.

“Yep,” Connie agreed. “I’ve got my pea coat and some coco for those usual winter temps in the mountains,” she concluded and headed to the break room. It was mid-50s in Garrison but the temperature would drop 20-30 degrees in the mountains.   She grabbed her big coat with gloves in the pockets, a knit cap, and thermos from her locker.   After retrieving them, she proceeded to boil water in a coffee maker for her coco.

Connie strolled out to engine 24 with her coat over one arm and thermos in the other hand. Stepping into the cab, she was humming “I saw Three Ships.” It was time to get this train moving. After securing her coat and thermos in the cab, she released the brakes on the locomotive and tender, moved the Johnson bar foreword of center, put one hand on the throttle, and the other on the automatic brake lever that would release the cars. Opening the throttle just enough to put tension on the cars, she then released the brakes to pull out the slack between the cars. She continued to open the throttle as the train started its motion forward. #24 gave a chug… and a chug… and a chug, as it moved slowly, pulling each coupling between cars taught, one at a time each one pulling against the engine, adding tension.   Each knuckle clanking with a jolt as more weight from the next car was added.

Chug, clang… chug, clang…
BANG! HISSSSSSSSSSSS
Connie almost jumped out of her boots at the loud noise but immediately cut the throttle, centered the Johnson bar, and reengaged the brakes to the engine & cars. She checked the gauges and the boiler pressure was dropping like a rock. She looked out the left side of the cab where she heard the noise and saw steam jetting out from the front left side. She hopped out to investigate what had happened and saw Charlie jogging up.

"Miss Connie, what's going on?" Charlie asked.

"I'm not sure," Connie bemused.

"Look there, it's the valve to the cylinder."   He observed staring at the valve assembly on top of the cylinder. "Looks like it totally blew out."

"Oh no," she said disheartened. "Do you think water got into the dry pipe?"

"Won't know until I take it apart."

"Can you fix it?"

"Sure but it's going to take time," he stated matter of factly.

"How long?"

"By myself? Eight hours at least. First, the firebox and boiler have to cool down. Then, I have to take apart the entire assembly. That's the rods, piston, cylinder, rings, slide valve, the works."

"And with help?" Connie queried.

"With a good hand, it would knock off three, maybe four hours," Charlie answered, "but I'm the only one here today. It's Christmas Eve so good luck trying to call someone in."

"Well then, I'll help you," Connie offered.

"Oh Miss Connie, I appreciate the offer but I don't think it really would make that much of a difference."

"Anything is better than eight hours! That would put the first stop in the wee hours of the morning at best," Connie said with a deflated spirit. "That's going to be too late for people to put presents under their tree and get their Christmas dinner."

"And how much of a difference would three more hours be?   #24 just isn't going to make it today," Charlie plainly said. "Also, sorry to say, without the experience, your help wouldn't take as much time off the job as a trained, experienced mechanic. I'd say you're better off trying to see if there are any other engines available."

With that suggestion, Connie's spirit lifted. This is a train depot after all; 24 isn't the only engine. Any diesel locomotive could pull the Christmas train up Cheyenne Pass and Connie was qualified to drive them as well. It wouldn't be the same tradition. It may be a mismatch and unexpected when it arrived but whatever got the job done.

"Of course," she exclaimed in a eureka moment. "Thanks, Charlie!" then ran to grab her coat out of the cab. She had to check with Hank and Alice immediately.

"I'll get Dutch to move 24 back into the roundhouse so I can get started on it. I'll put whatever overtime I need to get it going as soon as possible," Charlie said as she jumped into the cab.

"'Preciate it," she hollered back as she stuck her head out the window of the cab. Then she jumped back onto the loading dock platform.

"What happened?" Hank asked as he was walking out to see what had happen after hearing the commotion.

"Cylinder valve!   24 is out of commission!   Can you help me find another engine?" Connie was rambling and ran up to him.   "Like, put the word out to other stations and depots.   Tell them it's a Christmas emergency!"

"Connie, I'll do what I can because I know what this means to you," Hank stated, "but I don't want you to get your hopes up."

"Hank, it's Christmas.   It's *the* time for hope and miracles," she proclaimed and bolted off to see Alice.

"Alice!"   Connie ran to the office window in the breezeway.   Dropping her pea coat, she jumped up with her hands on the window counter like she was lifting herself out of a pool, "can you give me a copy of today's schedule?"   Scanning Alice's big board, she was trying to get an idea of the situation.   She would be able to see everything on the board but wanted a copy to take with her.

"Sure dear," the dispatcher said looking up from her chair.   It was probably the first time ever she looked up at Connie.   "What's going on?" she inquired.

"Cylinder valve blew. I need another engine," Connie panted.

"Is that what I heard out there? Oh no. No one was hurt, were they?"

"Everyone is fine except for my engine."

"I hope you can convince someone to help you, " the dispatcher sighed as she handed Connie a printed schedule. She sounded sincere enough but not very optimistic.

"I'll figure something out," Connie declared as she let herself down from the window counter, grabbed the schedule, then turned and ran off. It didn't matter to Connie how Alice felt. Connie saw two options on the board that were at the Garrison depot. The passenger terminal was closer, so she headed that way looking for the Gold Comet train.

A few minutes later, she was at the passenger terminal looking for the conductor. The Gold Comet passenger train had pulled into the terminal about fifteen minutes earlier and was terminating in Garrison today. Most of the crowd had already left the station. Some people were still collecting their bags or conversing with those they came to meet. Connie made her way up to the locomotive where she identified the conductor by his uniform. The engine was a big impressive machine, painted shiny gold. The conductor wore a well fitted suit and had a big bushy mustache.   He was talking with the engineer and she saw his name tag said "Carlos".

"Excuse me, merry Christmas, I hate to interrupt, mister… Carlos I see. I'm Connie," she introduced herself, "and I drive the #24 steam engine that takes the Christmas train over Cheyenne Pass."

"Oh yeah, I know about that tradition. You don't ride the rails around here at this time of year and not know about it," Carlos responded. He had a friendly enough expression but his by the book tone implied, "get to the point."

"Well, #24 has had an unfortunate breakdown," she continued, "I'm looking for a little Christmas miracle," she indicated with her thumb and forefinger, "and I need to ask if you can let the Gold Comet be used to get the Christmas train over the pass."

"Oh no, no, no," the bushy mustached man shook his head, "that wouldn't be possible."

Connie held up the copy of the schedule, "But the Gold Comet isn't going anywhere until late tomorrow afternoon. It's got more than enough power; the Christmas train is light. It's not that far and can be back in plenty of time."

"It's not that. I'm not going to have anyone work extra hours on short notice on Christmas Eve." The engineer standing next to Carlos was laughing under his breath at the fact this little girl would think to ask this.

"You don't have to; I'm licensed," she countered. "Also, think of the publicity," Connie had prepared this argument, "the Gold Comet saves Christmas!" she proclaimed while holding her hands, thumbs out and forefingers up as if to frame a newspaper headline.

"No ma'am," Carlos said emphatically, "the insurance wouldn't let us do it. As unlikely as it may be, if anything happened while this locomotive was pulling anything but Gold Comet passenger cars, the insurance would never cover it. It's too much of a liability for the company. Sorry, missy."

"But-"

"There's no way, Connie," he dismissed and leaned forward a bit. Then he curtly waved a hand in the air to cut off any further words from her and walked off with the engineer, not looking back. It seemed like the two had immediately forgotten about Connie. Either that or their conversation had shifted to the topic of "Can you believe that girl?"

Connie balled up her fists, stomped a foot, and pouted. She looked around at the remaining passengers now leaving the platform. No one paid her any mind.

Okay then, there was another she could ask. She took off running for the freight terminal to find the North-Union.

When she got there, she saw a dozen or so men in yellow hardhats bustling about. She asked the first one she passed, "Excuse me, who's in charge?"

"Vinny's the foreman. He's over there," the man pointed to the only blue hardhat.

Connie approached and asked, "Ho, ho, ho, merry Christmas. You must be Vinny."

The big bellied man barely glanced away from the clipboard he was staring at and replied while continuing to make marks on it with a pencil.

"Yeah, whadda want?"

"I'm Connie, the engineer that's taking the Christmas train up Cheyenne pass and-"

"**Hey, Joey!** Don't forget to bleed those air lines," Vinny looked up sharply and shouted at one of the men who appeared ready to step away from the North-Union train. "I don't need those brakes froze up when we come back after Christmas."

"Oh, right boss, I'm on it," the man shouted back.

Vinny went back to his clipboard.

"As I was saying," Connie resumed, "I'm moving the Christmas train-"

"Oh yeah, takes stuff up in the mountains every year," Vinny said with a touch of annoyance in his tone, only glancing momentarily at her from his clipboard. "What's that got to do with me?"

"Well," Connie started again, this time with some lighthearted laughter and slight comical gesticulations in an attempt to lighten the mood and soften the foreman up, "my old steamer, #24, blew a cylinder valve and is outta commission."

"Gee, that's too bad," the foreman mumbled.

"Yeah, I know, right? I mean, go figure," Connie said facetiously and rolled her eyes. "So, I was hoping for some fellow Christmas spirit to overcome this Christmas emergency and make a Christmas miracle happen."

"So what is it yous think I can do?" Vinny asked impatiently.

"Since the North-Union won't be running for the next couple of days," she held up the copy of the schedule, "I figured the locomotive can take the Christmas train over Cheyenne pass."

"Whadda ya crazy?!" Vinny finally looked away from his clipboard at her. "No way, no how!"

"I know you think I'm crazy but this is really important. The Christmas train has never failed in 50 years!" she pleaded turning her tone serious.

Vinny put the clipboard under his arm, "Look little lady, yous know what the union would do to me? As it is, I gotta get everybody outta here in the next 45 minutes or start shellin' out double overtime." The foreman started to walk off but Connie followed him, not giving up that easily.

"But the Christmas train has presents and food that need to get there tonight. You'd be saving Christmas."

"Listen, this is a union place. Any change in schedule with less than a week's notice, that's extra bucks we gotta give 'em," the foreman said as he motioned with the clipboard to the men in yellow hardhats. "On top of that, there's extra holiday pay."

"Can't you ask any of your engineers? And I really don't need one anyone anyhow," she continued to make her case. "I'm an engineer; I can drive it."

"First off little lady, yous ain't with the union," he countered. "Second, even if I could get an engineer to do it for the extra cash, the company ain't gonna authorize cuttin' that kinda paycheck, not in a million years, not for no Christmas train." Vinny waved his arms in a sweeping motion in front of himself, "Fuggedaboutit!"

"Maybe one will volunteer, without the pay, you know, because it's Christmas," she said now begging. That got Vinny to stop, turn, and this time, really look at her.

"Look, Connie, I feel for yous, I truly do," he said honestly as he put his hand on his heart. She wasn't getting the financial truth. He realized the only way to get this girl to stop, was to get to the emotional truth. "Yous talking 'bout Christmas and all. Well, everybody here has their own plans for Christmas and it involves going home, spending time wid their family and friends, watching their kids tomorrow openin' up what Santa's gonna bring 'em tonight. Capisce?"

Connie let out a sigh and her shoulders sank. She could tell his empathy was genuine.

"Look kid, I'm sorry, the people over the pass are just gonna have deal with the delay. If the train don't get up there 'til tomorrow or, uh, what is it, Boxing Day, they'll be all right." After finishing, Vinny snapped back into former mood.

"Okay, get off my case about all this. Yous starting to sound like my brudduh in law, always asking for some'in'." The foreman then turned to a group of yellow hardhats and shouted, "Come on guys, chop chop! Everybody wanna get home for Christmas, right? Let's wrap it up here."

Connie stood there and stared for a few moments. None of the men under yellow hardhats looked at her and they went about their business. Then Connie slowly turned and started back to her own loading dock shoving her hands in the pockets of her dungaree pants. As she passed the massive and imposing looking North-Union diesel locomotive, she glared at it. It wasn't shiny like the Comet, in fact, it was dirty but probably bigger. She looked back to where she was walking.

Hank! He must've made some phone calls. Maybe he pulled some strings with another depot in the area. He had to have come up with something. She started jogging.

By the time she got to the depot manager's office, Connie was at a full run and out of breath. She burst through the door without knocking. Hank was at his desk, looking down and slowly hanging up the phone. Before she could ask, he looked up, and shook his head.

"I've got nothing, Connie."

Her hand dropped off the door knob and she trudged in. Hank stood up and walked around his desk.

"I called every depot and station I could. No one is willing to send an engine over for the Christmas run," he said.

"Ugh!" her hands went to her head and she squeezed her eyes shut, "I can't believe this!" Then she dropped her hands and walked over to the window, staring out at the town of Garrison.

"I know what it means to you Connie but you've gotta understand how everyone else sees it," he began to explain. "In the grand scheme of things, it's just not a priority. Everyone has their own plans for Christmas. The Christmas run over Cheyenne pass is more tradition than anything. If it doesn't get there until tomorrow, sure, people will be upset but in the end, they'll get their gifts. It's not like we're asking to borrow an engine for immediate disaster relief or evacuate a town because of a forest fire."

Connie knew this but still couldn't believe the spirit of Christmas wasn't enough.

"You should go home now," Hank suggested. "I've got a few things to finish up here myself. Charlie said he'll work on 24 until it's done; no doubt Dela will bring him something to eat and coffee. You can come in as early as you like in the morning and get that load into the mountains. As for tonight, why don't you come over for supper? Mandy will be happy to make an extra plate."

Hank's office was on the second floor and she was staring out at the city, right over Old Ben parked out front. She was looking right over the answer to her prayers. Then she realized it.

"Hank…" she slowly said in a low volume.

"What is it?" he asked and knitted his brow.

She spun around to face him, eyes wide and her fingertips went to her forehead. "I should've thought of it before! Heck, I should've thought of it first!"

"What are you talking about?" Hank sputtered with confusion.

She pointed out the window with her eyes still locked on Hank's, "Old Ben! #307! It still works, I can pull the train with it!"

"Connie, no," Hank put his hands up.

"We take it out twice a year, for July 4th and Pioneer Day." Connie stretched out her arms and asked, "Why not?!"

"It's past a hundred years old and hasn't actually pulled a load in over thirty" Hank explained.

"But it's the same class as #24," she came back.

"You remember two Pioneer Days ago when it had to be towed back because it threw a piston rod," he reminded her, "and that was just the loop around town without cars."

"Yeah but Charlie replaced it."

"And three 4th of Julys ago when Old Ben didn't even go because the boiler wouldn't hold pressure?"

"Which Charlie also fixed."

"Connie, the point is I don't know what's going to go out on Old Ben next or when," the depot manager said. "That's why it's a museum piece now. I wouldn't feel comfortable with 307 doing a real run unless Charlie thoroughly inspected it, it went out on a shakedown run on flat, open track, then a re-inspection."

"Hank, don't you give up on me too," she came back in a desperate tone, "I'll take the risk. Besides, what's the worst that can happen? Old Ben breaks on the way and we're no worse off. Isn't it worth it to save Christmas?"

"It's not Old Ben I'm worried about. It's you!" Hank said with great concern. "The worst that can happen is you'll be stuck in the mountains, in the tunnel or Horseshoe Shelf, over night in freezing winter mountain weather with help hours away."

"I'll…" Connie thought for a moment then said, "bring a blanket just in case." She was running out of arguments.

"Not to mention, blocking Cheyenne Pass for who knows how long until I could get an engine to clear it," Hank concluded. "I'm not going to put you in that situation. Besides, your dad would kill me." That was the final word on the subject. Connie was defeated and looked down at the floor.

Hank put a hand on her shoulder and said, "Go home and I'll see you tonight for supper. No one is going to blame you for this."

She slowly walked out of the office and downstairs. She plodded downstairs, shuffled out front, and stared at Old Ben, all decked out with its decorations. The plaque next to it explained the history of engine 307. In its day, it was a true workhorse and as shiny as it was on the outside, polished up as a museum piece. Hank was right. Ben was sixty years older than #24 and its condition was questionable. She still would've taken it, no matter what the risk, if she could convince Hank but she knew his mind was made up.

She turned and walked back through the breezeway to the dock. She stood and stared at the Christmas train. #24's coal tender was still attached but the locomotive had been pulled away. The 50th anniversary, her first time driving it, and it would be the first time it wouldn't make it on Christmas Eve. No presents for some kids come Christmas morning; no special meals for some families on Christmas Day. True, those who had food being delivered wouldn't starve and most would simply have to make do with meals that weren't nearly as special but everyone deserves a good, special feast on Christmas Day. Mainly, it was the kids. She thought of herself as a child waiting on Christmas Eve with her parents at the station in O'Neill and seeing it pull in. Her grandparents, aunts, and uncles all sent their presents on the train. She thought about the five decades of kids who would wait for the train every Christmas. Kids who now had children and grandchildren of their own. Parents who, as kids, received gifts from the train that wouldn't see their kids get presents from it this year. She turned back to the depot building, sat down on a bench, dropped her face into her hands, her long dark hair falling down in front, and she was about to start crying.

She heard an engine bell behind her in the distance, the signal that an engine was pulling into the roundhouse. Connie knew it was #24 being put in for Charlie to work on. The sound just made her think about it more, which made her more depressed.

Then she sat up, not quickly, not slowly; she just sat upright as a thought entered her head.   What was moving #24 into the roundhouse?

She turned to look over her shoulder in the direction of the roundhouse. It was the little switcher engine; it had just pushed #24 into the roundhouse. The switcher was sticking out of the bay. Charlie had it in the center bay, which was lined up directly with the line leading into the roundhouse so the turntable didn't have to pivot. Connie turned back to the depot building and with a blank expression, stared off into space through her dark locks that still draped in front of her face as a couple questions formed in her mind.

How much horsepower…?

I wonder what the top speed…?

Connie brushed her hair back behind her ears, stood up, and turned around to face the roundhouse. The switcher was a short, stubby little 0-6-0 steamer, only three drive axles, no lead or trail axles.

"Who was it that Charlie said was working the switcher today?" she asked to herself as she cocked her head to the side. Dutch.   She didn't know Dutch too well, speaking in passing here and there but that was a lot more interaction than she had had with Carlos or Vinny before today. The switcher started to move out of the roundhouse area and Connie had to push any hope that might start to resurge back down deep inside her. She couldn't take getting her hopes back up, only to be dashed again. With her arms hanging by her side, she flattened her hands and spread her fingers.

"Okay Connie," she told herself under her breath, "just ask what it can do," and she moved out with a purpose, jumping off the loading dock, crossing the tracks towards the little switcher engine.

Dutch had the switcher moving at a walking pace and rolling off the turntable when someone shouting startled him.

"Hey Dutch!"

"Huh?" he looked to his right and down. Standing on the ladder to the cab, now riding along was the petite little Christmas train engineer. "Oh hey, Connie."

"What's up?" as she climbed up even with the deck but still hanging on the outside of the cab.

"Not much.   Sorry about #24," he mentioned as he pointed with his thumb over his shoulder back at the roundhouse.

"Yeeeaaah," she drew out.   "I was just wondering, how much horsepower does this switcher have?"

"650 or there about," he said not looking away from the controls.

"And what kinda torque does it put out?" she continued to probe.

"7,000 foot pounds at the low RPMs."

"Gee, with that kinda power, how fast could it get up to?"

"Oh on its own, it could probably do 60, maybe 65 miles an hour if there was a reason." Then he queried, "Why you ask?"

"Oh I just love these old steam engines and I never really looked at #12 and since I saw it and you and I wasn't going anywhere, I figured I'd ask a little about it."   Connie thought for a moment.   If the Christmas train cars were anything more than what they were, there would be no way but with what Dutch just told her, that should just about do it.   Still, she tried to stifle the hope that was fighting its way back up inside her.

"Sooo…" she drew out, "whatcha got going on now?" she asked as she stepped into the cab.

"I was about to park #12 here, clock out, and head home," he turned his head to her. "All I really had to do today was move some oilers. Makes for not even half a day's work and get outta here early for Christmas Eve- oh, and move 24, but that didn't take long."

"Sooo… could I use this to move something?" Connie eased into the question but quickly added, "You don't have to stay, I can run it. I don't want to hold you up on Christmas Eve."

"Ah, it's no big deal. It's my job," Dutch stated. "I can move one more thing before clocking out. How long could it take? Whatcha need?"

"Oh," Connie rolled her eyes up, "I just need to move the Christmas train."

"Yeah sure, no problem," he said. "You need it off the loading dock and where to?"

"Oh, not far. You know… just, kinda, over Cheyenne Pass," she said turning her head away and trailing off as she said the words "Cheyenne Pass".

"Yeah, you got it- HEY! Wait! What?!" Dutch hit the brakes on #12 when "Cheyenne Pass" actually sank into his brain. The engine jolted to a stop and Connie had to brace herself.

"You said over Cheyenne Pass?!" he incredulously inquired.

"Okay, forget I said that!" she blurted out holding up her hands. Connie realized her tactical error. She should've stayed vague and say she only needed to move the train, not say where. She then quickly rattled off, "Look, just clock out and go home and enjoy Christmas. All you need to tell anyone, if they ask, is I wanted to move the Christmas train off the loading dock."

"You must have kangaroos loose in the top paddock because that's crazy," was his reaction.

"From what I know of Cheyenne pass and the Christmas train, which is everything there is to know mind you, and what you just told me about engine 12, it should have enough tractive effort to get the job done," the little engineer petitioned.

"You're telling me, you think this switcher engine, little number 12, can pull a load up through Cheyenne Pass?" Dutch wanted to confirm.

"Yes," she said confidently, "I think this little engine can."

He paused a few moments, then reflected, "You really are serious about this, aren't you?"

The young woman took a step towards Dutch and glared up, right into his eyes.

Dutch was lightly built and only average height for a man but standing toe to toe, short Connie was looking straight up at him.

After another few moments of thinking, Dutch knew he had to tell her something. Still believing this idea was ludicrous, he took off his baseball hat, ran his hand through his short, dirty blonde hair, and said, "All right, if you want to do this, we're going to have to game plan it."

Back in the break room, Dutch unrolled a railroad map on the table.

"Tell me about Cheyenne Pass," he said.

"There's almost 20 miles between the depot and where the incline starts. There's even a slight downgrade after the depot heading to Miller's Creek, that'll help get the train going. I figure that's got to be enough of a running start to get over the mountain."

"How long is the incline and how steep is the grade?"

"About five miles and the grade maxes out at 8%."

"That's a tall order for #12."

"But if it can get up to 50-55 mph, that'll be enough momentum and that's got to be enough room to do it."

"I don't think that little guy has ever gotten that fast."

"You said it could do over 60," she retorted.

"On it's own, without cars, on flat track" he countered.

"Well I'm not asking to do 60. 50, with only 12 cars that aren't nearly maxed out on weight and a long running start," Connie made her case. "There's no reason it can't," she held out her arms.

"Okay, *if* it can get up to that speed and up that incline, what's after that?" Dutch asked looking at the map with his thumbs in the belt loops of his jeans.

"Not long after the start of the incline, is where the tunnel begins," Connie explained as she traced the tracks on the map with her finger. "Once the end of the tunnel is in sight, that's where the tracks level out and from there it shouldn't be a problem. About a half mile out of the tunnel is the switch to turn north onto Horseshoe Shelf. Straight would take you southwest over Monarch Gorge."

"After Horseshoe Shelf, what's this Pearson Ridge like?" Dutch inquired, pointing to the map.

"That's nothing compared to the Cheyenne tunnel," she dismissed leaning on the table with her hands. "It's not nearly as long and the max grade is only 5 & a half percent."

"That's still pretty steep. How fast can you go around Horseshoe Shelf?" he scratched his two day stubble as he continued to probe.

"I take it at 20 mph to be safe; certainly wouldn't go over 25," she said as she turned to look at him wondering why he asked.

"It's just that it doesn't look like a lot of room to build more speed after the bend and before you hit the incline for Pearson Ridge," Dutch said flatly as he crossed his arms.

Connie then knew why he asked about the speed on the Shelf. She stood up straight, scrunched her nose, and let out a pouty snort. She could've kicked Dutch for being negative but she knew he was right to point it out. Connie had been so fixed on getting up the big incline through the tunnel, she completely dismissed Pearson Ridge. It wasn't as long or steep but with no room to build up speed, it could be a bigger problem.

"Okay," she started thinking out loud, "it's not as bad as it seems. I can take Horseshoe Shelf at 25 and I know once I see the third car back come from behind the cliff on the Shelf, that's when the tracks start to straighten out. It's right about here," she pointed to spot on the curve in the track going north. "Right there I can pour on the steam. I don't have to wait for the tracks to straighten out completely to start accelerating."

Dutch's eyebrows raised and he pushed his baseball hat back a little. She was right. The train only needed to hold back its speed at the tightest part of the turn. Looking at the map, it gave significantly more room to pick up speed from where she pointed. Still, it would be tight.

"All right then, let me get my coat and watch cap," and he turned to his locker. "It's cold in the mountains."

"What?" she asked not believing what she just heard.

"I'm not letting you do this on your own," he said plainly as he grabbed his coat and wool knit cap. Turning back to her, he continued, "I visited my family down in Phoenix for Thanksgiving; I've got no one coming to see me this Christmas. Why do you think I'm here today? Besides, you could probably use a fireman."

Connie's gut reaction was to tell him off. This was her time, her mission. But an instant later a smile slowly crept onto her face and turned into the biggest smile Dutch had ever seen. Even if he wasn't completely convinced this was possible with little engine #12, she had found someone that believed in her enough to be on her side and back her up. The Christmas spirit was still alive.

"Let's do this!" she exclaimed.

First, she had to catch Alice. Connie ran to the dispatch office and saw Alice locking the door to her office.

"Alice," she panted as she paused just long enough to say, "before you go, make the call and tell everyone in the mountains we may be running late but the Christmas train is coming!" Connie then bolted towards the rails yelling over her shoulder, "I found an engine!"

"Oh," was all Alice said with a look of bewilderment as Connie left.

Dela walked into the roundhouse with a pair of BLT sandwiches in a brown bag and a thermos of coffee for her husband as he worked on #24.

"Brought you a little something to keep you going, my honey," she announced.

"You know, I probably would've starved 40 years ago if it weren't for you," Charlie said gratefully.

"You know you a saint for staying here and fixing this thing up," she said as she set the brown bag and thermos down on a work bench.

"I just feel bad for Miss Connie," he said. "It just wouldn't be right to not do something."

"Just don't be too late, honey dear," Dela said. "I'll be waiting at home under the mistletoe for ya."

"Well, I better get back to it then."

"You know, walking over here, I saw the dangedest thing," she changed up the subject.

"What's that?" Charlie asked.

"Dutch and that child, Connie, hooking up the yard switcher to the Christmas train," she explained.

"What're they doing that for? She should know those cars don't need to be moved from the loading dock," he wondered aloud. Then it hit him.

"Uh-oh! Miss Connie is just crazy enough to try it."

Connie and Dutch had backed up engine 12 and hooked it up to the waiting coal tender in front of the rest of the cars on the loading dock. As a switcher, it typically didn't use a tender but they were going to need the coal for this. They connected the brake lines and Dutch stepped back into the cab and to the left. He held out his hand, offering her the spot on the right where the engineer controls and seat were.

"It's your show. Go ahead and take the reins," he said.

She grinned and he helped her on board with is other hand. The boiler was at operating pressure. The air brakes on the cars were fully charged. She put the Johnson bar forward, opened up the throttle, and released the brakes to the cars and locomotive. With chug after chug, the engine pulled out the slack from the cars and the train slowly started to move forward. Connie was radiant as she moved the Johnson bar all the way forward to give the locomotive as much torque as possible. Slowly but surely, they were on their way.

"What do you mean 'she found an engine'?" Hank asked Alice in the parking lot. They had parked next to each other and met by their cars on their way out.

"That's all she said and ran off," she replied.   "I figured she had coordinated something with you."

Hank stared blankly at Alice, then he started jogging back to the depot.

As the little engine started to pick up tempo, the two occupants heard a voice shout out from the left side of the engine.

"Miss Connie! Mister Dutch!" Charlie called out. They looked out to the left, just behind the cab of the engine and saw Charlie running with a brown paper bag in his outstretched hand. "Here's something for the road!"

Dutch stepped out on the left side ladder and grabbed the sandwiches with a smile of appreciation. Connie put her hands to the sides of her mouth and shouted back, "Thanks Charlie!" then waved vigorously with a smile.

"Good luck!" he yelled back.

Hank stepped out onto the platform in time to see the Christmas train clear the station and his jaw dropped. Connie was using the switcher to take the train into the mountains. It was still moving slow but just fast enough and far enough to not be caught now. She was right not to have asked him about using #12. Hank would've locked her in his office or chained her to a telephone pole to stop her. This was insane! He should've been mad; he should've been irate; he should've been livid. He wanted to be angry but he couldn't. He couldn't be mad at Connie for finding a way to do what she had always wanted to do. So he just stood there and put his hands on his hips, staring in surreal disbelief at the departing westbound train. He was going to be worried sick until he got word that the train made it.   And if it didn't, he would probably have a heart attack.

A few hundred feet down the tracks, the last car passed Charlie and he came into Hank's view. The two just looked at each other across the distance and the old mechanic simply shrugged his shoulders, arms out and palms up, as he looked back at the depot manager standing on the dock.

"Fifteen miles an hour," Dutch said, looking at the speed gage. The several miles of slight downgrade towards Miller's Creek is where they were going to have to get most of their momentum. She looked out the right side as they came up to a crossing. A flatbed pickup truck loaded with hay stopped as the guard arms came down. She pulled on the lanyard and let out two long blasts of the train whistle as they approached the crossing. The driver of the pickup wore a cowboy hat and stuck his arm out his window to wave. Smiling, she waved back and yelled, "Merry Christmas!" even though the man in the truck probably couldn't hear.

"Twenty miles per hour," Dutch reported.

"If we get to 40 by the time we cross Miller's Creek, we should be good," Connie proclaimed. "I'll bet we can make 45."

"You might be right but can we get another ten on top of that before the incline starts?" he questioned.

"Have some Christmas faith," was her response. Grinning widely she let out another couple of short blasts from the whistle.

As the single trestle bridge over Miller's Creek came into view in the distance, Dutch dug into the bag Charlie handed off to him and took a bite out of one of the sandwiches.

"Might as well eat these now," he said with a mouth full of BLT as he handed her the other one.

"Good ol' Charlie," she replied and took the sandwich. "I'll have to thank him and Dela when we get back." They were taking in the scenery of farmland, watching the mountains grow bigger in front of them, and monitoring the speedometer.

"Coming up to 35 mph," Dutch said. The acceleration was slow but steady.

"Normally I pull back the Johnson bar before here to a cruising setting," she told him, "but we're going to have to accelerate this whole way."

A little while later, Dutch could see a man and boy fishing in the creek as they approached the single trestle bridge. The two at the creek waved to the engine. Dutch waved back as Connie gave another long blow of the whistle. Dutch had to smile now. Connie's spunkiness was becoming infectious.

Crossing the Miller Creek bridge, he looked at the speed gage. It was just over the 40 mph hash mark. "I'd say 41 miles an hour," he stated.

"It'll do," Connie came back.

They were just over halfway to the start of the upgrade and gotten most of the speed they were going to need but now they were out of the slight downgrade that was helping them.

"Yeah but at these faster speeds, there's less time for pressure to build in the cylinders," he voiced his concern. He almost continued, "and this little guy simply wasn't built for speed," but he kept that to himself. Still, the needle on the speed gage kept creeping clockwise, although it was moving slower now. It was so slow, they couldn't tell it was moving from a glance; they had to give it a minute or two to notice a change in the needle's position.

"Fifty miles an hour," Dutch shouted over the increase in noise some time later.

"All right!" Connie exclaimed. "Let's see how much more this little guy can get before the grade."

"I'll throw some more coal in." Dutch opened the firebox, stepped to the tender, and tossed in a few shovels full of coal.

There was an old farmhouse that Connie used as a marker. It was exactly one mile from the start of the upgrade and it just came into sight.

They passed the farmhouse and Connie held her head out the right side of the cab, closed her eyes, and felt the wind. Dutch closed up the firebox, looked up at her, and saw her long, dark brown hair in the wind. He just stared at her for several moments, then chuckled to himself.

"I don't believe it," he remarked after turning back to the gages.

"What is it?" she asked as she pulled her head back inside and back to earth.

"We're at about 52 miles per hour," he said surreally and tapped the gauge as if he was seeing things.

"EEEYES!" Connie shouted. "We're going to do this!" then glanced outside again. "We're starting the incline."

Dutch was now increasing the odds of success in his head. He didn't have it at 100%

but it was closer to that than it was when they left the station. The tunnel was dead ahead.

As the upgrade started, there was no immediate noticeable decrease in speed. Dutch engaged the dynamo so the various lights in the cab could be turned on before entering the tunnel.

"This is where it's going to start to get uncomfortable," Connie stated. "When we enter the tunnel is where I normally close the side curtains to keep out the cold but this little guy doesn't have them."

"Good thing I brought my coat," Dutch replied.

As they entered the tunnel, cold air invaded the cab. Connie was putting her coat on and Dutch checked the speedometer. It had dropped below 50.

"Now we'll see if that was enough momentum," he cried out over the echoing noise in the tunnel.

"I think it is," she shouted back, "heck, I know it is!"

The angle of attack increased as the speed continued to bleed off. Right at the point where the grade was steepest, at 8%, the needle on the speed gage was dropping the fastest and Dutch got worried.

"We're under 30 miles an hour now," he announced.   There was still plenty of uphill track to go.

"It's all right," she assured him. "This is where the grade starts to level out."   She instinctively knew where they were in the tunnel.

Sure enough, the momentum of the gage's needle started to slow but it was still dropping.

"Twenty," came another report from Dutch.

"We're almost there," she declared as she stared out the right side waiting to see the light at the end of the tunnel.

"Fifteen,"   The needle kept moving counter clockwise and the strokes of the pistons had become labored.

"Just a little further," she cried out over the reverberating sounds and still glaring out.

"Dropping under 10 miles per hour!" Dutch yelled. He glanced out of the cab at the tracks below and knew he could run faster than this.

"That's it!" Connie reveled and looked back in the cab at Dutch. "I see the end of the tunnel. We're gonna to make it!"

Dutch stared back at the speed gage. It was under the 10mph hash mark but it had stopped moving; he figured they were doing seven, maybe eight miles per hour. The piston strokes were slow but in a steady rhythm. They seemed to be stronger strokes now, not as labored as just a few moments ago. Then the needle started to move again, ever so slowly. This time in the clockwise direction.

"I'll be," he called out with a grin, then a laugh. He looked out the left side of the cab at the approaching light that was growing bigger and getting brighter. He looked back over at Connie. She was sitting in the engineer's seat staring back with the most satisfying smile imaginable. Dutch gave a smile back that conveyed, "You were right." After a little while, he looked back at the speedometer.

"Fifteen miles per hour," he said. "One incline down; one to go."

"Let's get this baby back up to 25 miles an hour and get ready for Pearson Ridge," she said excitedly and blew the whistle as they left the tunnel.

"Passing 20 miles an hour now," Dutch said with some relief but was now thinking of Pearson Ridge. Could little #12 do it again?

Connie looked out of the cab once more. This time looking for the switch ahead where the tracks split: straight, continuing south-west over Monarch Gorge and to the right, turning to the north around Horseshoe Shelf.

She saw the switch signal about half a mile ahead.

"That's funny..." she said to herself. The signal didn't look right. She squinted to see better. As she stared at the switch signal and as it got closer, she saw what was wrong and complete panic hit her.

"OH NO!" Connie shot into the cab and threw the throttle back, killing the power.

"What's wrong?" Dutch asked, completely bemused at her tone of voice and actions, now seeing her reach for the brakes.

"The switch is in the wrong position!" urgently explaining as she pulled both brake levers for the engine and cars. "If we don't stop, we'll head over the Gorge instead of around the Shelf!"

Dutch shuffled around her to look out the right side to see for himself and how far away they were. Sure enough, the switch signal showed it was in the straight position. Still, he didn't see the urgency.

"Well, if we can't stop in time, we'll just have to back up," he said.

"No, you don't get it!" Connie franticly expressed. "The incline goes back *down* over the Gorge! If we have to stop on or after the bridge, this engine might not be able to back up from a dead stop!"

Now Dutch got it and shared the gravity of the situation. He looked back at the speed gage. They were just slowing under 15 mph. He looked back to the switch and judged less than a quarter mile to it. First he was worried they would slow down too much in the tunnel; now he didn't think they would slow down fast enough. He looked at the ground, judged the speed, and jumped.

He hit the ground running but stumbled and struggled to stay on his feet. Once he got his footing, Dutch sprinted as fast as he could to get in front of the locomotive with enough space to turn the switch manually. Connie kept a hand on each of the two brake levers as the train screeched to slow down. Dutch passed the front of the engine and kept going for all he was worth. He didn't look back but was getting more and more distance between him and the engine. He reached the switch and hurriedly fumbled with the pin to unlock the lever. Connie looked out to check on his progress. The train wasn't going to stop before the switch. Dutch frantically lifted the lever off the ground and forward moving the rails, aligning them to the right. As the lever reached straight up, he slipped on the gravel, falling forward with the lever onto the ground, completing the switch's movement as #12's wheels rolled into the switch.

The train wasn't even going five miles per hour now but Dutch hastily scrambled to his feet again to catch back up to the ladder of the cab. Connie released the brakes and reached out to help him back in the cab.

"You did it!" she praised him.

Panting furiously, unable to speak with one hand on a knee, he just waved his other hand back and forth between them, then finally got out, "We did it." She gave him a quick hug.

"When they heard the Christmas train wasn't coming, Estes Station probably left the switch in the straight position," she theorized, then turned back to the controls.

"Okay, let's get some speed back," she stated as she opened up the throttle again. The train began to slowly pick up speed anew and Connie went over to the left side of the cab. She gazed out over the Gorge. Dutch moved over to check the speedometer.

"Fifteen miles an hour," he said plainly. "Better get some more coal in the firebox." Connie reached back without breaking her trance out over Monarch Gorge and grabbed his arm.

"Wait!" she stopped him. He looked over to her and in a dreamy voice, she continued, "This is my favorite part."

He stepped behind her and looked over at the scenery. It was like something out of a fairytale picture book. The majestic Monarch Gorge was breathtaking. Snow sporadically covered the sides of the mountains. Rock cliffs rose up and pine trees lined the mountain tops where the slopes leveled off. Connie was definitely right to take this in, especially after their close call. They both needed the mental pause. It couldn't last for ever, just a minute or so. Dutch turned back to the speed gage and controls.

"Approaching 25 miles per hour. Better hold it back or Hank will be very upset that we spilled the Christmas train into the Gorge," he said as he pulled the Johnson bar back and let off the throttle some. Connie was quickly back in the game too, checking the water level and boiler pressure. Snow started to fall and the sun was setting making Dutch finally notice the cold. He had been so mentally occupied, it hadn't hit him until now and he put on his coat and switched his baseball hat for the watch cap.

Now for their next trick. Pearson Ridge. The fire was going to need stoking. Dutch stepped to the coal tender, grabbed the shovel, and collected a pile on the end of it. Connie opened the firebox as Dutch stepped back to the cab then tossed the coal in. He repeated the action twice more, shut the firebox door, and speared the shovel into the coal.

"Let me know as soon as you see car #3," Connie instructed as she put her hand on the throttle, ready to open it up as soon as Dutch gave the word. He stepped around her, out onto the right side ladder of the engine and looked back. The turn was tight and he waited for the third car to reappear from the cliffside, the sign they could start accelerating again. It would be any second now. The engine chugged and the wheels clacked on the tracks. Connie waited, one hand on the throttle, the other on the Johnson bar, head turned, staring at Dutch hanging outside, who was staring back at the cars. Then he shouted.

"Hit it!"

Connie threw the throttle wide open and jammed the Johnson bar all the way forward. "Come on little engine, let's go!" she encouraged the machine as Dutch climbed back in.

"We're getting some speed," Dutch commented and Connie looked outside for familiar landscape that indicated where the Ridge started. The tracks were surrounded by trees and she knew every one of them.

After a couple of minutes, she said, "Here comes the upgrade."

"We'll barely make 35 mph," Dutch replied. The needle strained to reach the 35mph mark on the speedometer, then held, no longer moving clockwise. He knew it was about to reverse direction again.

The snowfall was picking up and the speed began to drop. The piston strokes were getting labored once more. Each tree they passed went by slower than the previous one.

"Falling under 20 miles an hour," Dutch observed the speedometer. The frequency of the strokes continued to lower.

"You've got this number 12," Connie uttered, frustrated there was nothing else either of them could do but watch the momentum sink. Dutch thought there might actually be some doubt in her voice.

"How much farther until we're on flat ground again?" he asked. "Because we're about to go under ten."

"About half a mile," was her answer as she looked out to the right, judging the speed by the passing scenery. Under ten miles per hour, the speed gage was useless. It was more helpful to look at the ground and it was moving at a jogging pace.

"Don't let up now little guy, we're almost home free!" she pronounced in desperation.

They were at a quick walking pace when the next thing Dutch knew, Connie had jumped out of the cab onto the ground and started to push the engine herself.

"Just keep moving!" she growled. For what it was worth, she leaned with all her weight into the ladder of the locomotive as it groaned and slowly chugged.

"Well, what the hey," Dutch reacted and jumped down on the left side to do the same. As he pushed on the ladder, he uttered, "We've come this far, let's finish it!"

Ignoring the heavy snowfall, Connie and Dutch both dug their feet into the ground, pushing with every ounce of human strength they had. The quick walking pace became a regular pace, then a slow one as the machine and two people struggled against the remaining grade. The piston strokes were slow and extremely labored. The drive wheels started to slip a bit with each stroke.

"Ugh- *come on,* **come on!**" Connie let out.

"Keep going!" Dutch grumbled.

The train was now at a crawl. *"Oh please,* DON'T STOP NOW!" she pleaded and closed her eyes as a tear formed in each one. Their feet were barely moving.

It was like this for what seemed an hour but may only have been a minute and Connie thought she took one step shorter than the previous. She made sure to plant the next step deliberately. No, she hadn't taken that step too short because the next one was also slightly faster. Her steps weren't shorter, the pace was getting faster. Still slow but definitely not as slow.

"We're going faster!" she shouted with fevered excitement.

"We're not out of this yet," Dutch called back and the two continued to push.

In a few more moments, they were walking at a steady pace, slow but steady. The pace continued to pick up and before they realized it, they were walking briskly.

"WE'RE GOING TO MAKE IT!" Connie excitedly exclaimed. They both knew it and simultaneously jumped back onto their respective ladders.

Climbing back into the cab, she rushed Dutch and gave him a hug that took him off balance. He put an arm around her, steadied himself with the other on the window of the cab, and laughed. She broke the embrace, turned to the engine's controls, and leaned over them declaring, "I love you little engine!"

She would've put her arms all the way around engine #12 if they were long enough.

Connie shook her head and brushed the snow out of her hair. Dutch took off his watch cap and slapped it on his knee to get the snow out of it. As they brushed the snow off their jackets, her hands were shaking from the cold. The aching from the cold had finally hit her and Dutch noticed.

"Get your hands warm by the firebox," he said.

"Oh wait!" she had to do one thing before getting her hands warm. Connie reached up and pulled the train whistle lanyard letting out two long blasts. It was more than a celebratory gesture. People in Estes would be able to hear from where they were; she wanted them to know they were soon to arrive.

"First stop, Estes," she announced as she pulled the Johnson bar back some, then shuffled over to the firebox to get warm. "Running behind, they'll have to do with dropping the cars; we can't wait around for them to unload."

They slowed the train as it approached Estes Station and Connie hit the whistle again. There was a crowd waving and cheering as they pulled in and she stopped so the last two cars were centered on the platform.

"Just release the last two and well get on to Sundance," she shouted to the station manager on the platform. He jogged over to the couplers, disappeared between the cars for a moment, then stepped back out onto the platform, giving the engine crew a thumbs up. Waving to the people, they pulled out and onto the next town of Sundance. Repeating this process four more times to similar crowds, they were left with the last two cars and the last stop of the night.

"Onward to O'Neill!" Connie proclaimed as she raised an arm as if she was signaling a cavalry charge. She was absolutely beaming and couldn't wait to get to her hometown.

The snow was now falling in light flurries as they pulled into O'Neill Station. Connie eased the train in and stopped on the platform. As soon as it came to a complete halt, she stuck her head out the side and spotted who she was looking for.

"MOM! DAD!" she shouted and waved as the station manager and volunteer porters opened the cars up to start passing out the gifts. Connie jumped on the platform and ran to a middle aged couple, a blue collar type man of medium height and build with salt & pepper hair and a short petite brunette woman. The pair waved back and briskly stepped towards Connie. She hugged her parents simultaneously.   Her mother kissed her on the head; father patted her on the back.

"The Christmas train brought our favorite gift once again" her father said. "I can't believe you did it with that little locomotive and I can't believe Hank let you."

"Well… I might have some explaining to do with Hank," she knitted her brow, gritted her teeth, and shrugged her shoulders sheepishly. Recomposing herself, she turned and praised the engine, "but that little guy is a *champ!*" Dutch had stepped out onto the platform to see what was going on and Connie saw him.

"Oh, that's Dutch," she pointed out, returning to her folks. "I couldn't have done it without him." Waving Dutch over, she introduced him, "Dutch, this is my mom and dad." He walked over to the three and extended his hand.

"Good to meet you," her father took his hand with a firm shake.

"It's a pleasure," Connie's mother said with a friendly smile when Dutch shook her hand. "Have you been up here before? We have a new Nativity set in the town square."

"It's a big upgrade from the old, cheap, half sized plastic ones we had," her father added. Before Dutch could answer, Connie blurted out.

"Oh wait!" and she ran back to the first car. Stepping inside the railcar, it only took her a few seconds to find the box she had Louis put in and ran back out to her parents and Dutch with the box.

"I'll go show him. He hasn't seen it either," acknowledging that she hadn't seen the new set up herself.

The town square was essentially right next to the rail station and Connie was practically dragging Dutch, making their way through the crowd. They broke past the crowd at the station, hurried down a block, past a group of carolers and people simply taking in the Christmas atmosphere, then made a turn. Right there in the middle of the square were life-sized wooden figures of Mary, Joseph, shepherds, and animals, in a stable around a manger. All were magnificently painted. The snow covered streets and buildings with flurries continuing to fall all completed the perfect Christmas scene.

Dutch stopped short of the figures but Connie stepped right up to the manger, kneeled down, and opened the box. Brushing off some sawdust and pulling open a couple layers of packing paper, Connie gently removed a wood carved infant in swaddling cloth and placed it in the manger. She stood up, turned around, stared at Dutch for a moment, and spoke.

"Merry Christmas, Dutch."

"Merry Christmas, Con-" before he could finish, Connie had rushed forward and kissed him on the cheek.

Embarrassed, Connie withdrew quickly. She didn't know how that happened, as if some exterior force had taken her over for a heartbeat. Wide eyed, Dutch was somewhat lost and equally speechless. Blushing hard, she stammered after another moment.

"I'm sorry- uh, no, I mean…" she closed her eyes and a palm went to her forehead. "What I want to say is…" Connie dropped the hand back to her side after a long pause and her big doe eyes locked with Dutch. After another drawn out moment staring at each other, her head tilted slightly to the side, and she finally got out the word she was trying to say.

"Thanks."

Dutch finally collected himself and let out a small laugh, coming back with, "Anytime, Connie."

To the east where the sky wasn't covered by clouds, a shooting star caught both their eyes. They both stared off into the stars for awhile until Dutch finally turned to Connie.

"Is there a shop around here to buy a girl a cup of coffee?" he asked.

"How about a milkshake?" she responded as she turned to him sharply. "There's just enough time to hit McKenzie's ice cream shop before they close," she continued and took his hand to lead on.

"Milkshakes on a cold Christmas night?"

"Yeah, they have special flavors for the holidays: peppermint and pumpkin spice." She proposed, "You'll have to get one flavor, I'll get the other, then we can share so neither misses out."

As they walked and without realizing it, Connie leaned up against Dutch because of the cold. Dutch put his arm around her without thinking.

"Come to think of it, are there any inns around here?" he wondered aloud.

"Don't think of it. My parents have a spare room," she answered. "Since we're in no hurry to get the train back tomorrow, you can stay for our Christmas feast. You can meet my brothers; they'll be over too."

"Brothers?"

"Don't worry; they'll like you."

A few months later in early summer, the Garrison depot finally took delivery of a brand new diesel electric switcher engine and the old coal steamer, #12, was retired. However, instead of being scrapped as was originally planned, it found a new home out in front of the depot as a museum piece next to engine #307, Old Ben. It didn't take much convincing the powers that be to make it happen after the little engine's remarkable Christmas run.   It got its own plaque, explaining its history with a separate paragraph on how it saved Christmas on that 50th anniversary run. Also on the plaque, Hank had it named "Little Connie".   Every season, both engines got dressed up and decked out in Christmas decorations. Like Old Ben on July 4 & Pioneer Day, Little Connie would make a loop around town at Christmas time.

Connie & Dutch learned everything they needed to know about maintaining steam engines from Charlie before he retired and never let engine 24 go down again. But just in case, they always coordinated a backup plan with Hank for the Christmas run. Connie & Dutch continued to drive the Christmas train every year until finally, their own kids took it over.

About this Story

The Little Engine that Could is a timeless story about believing something seemingly impossible can be done and never giving up. As a dad of two boys who love everything typical boys love, trains are one of those things. I love watching them play with their wooden toy train set as much as they love actually playing with it. We like trains and on some level, who doesn't?

At some point after reading *The Little Engine that Could* to the boys again, I pondered how that scenario would play out in real life. In reality, if a train broke down, there probably would be no serious repercussions if it was late by one day with it's cargo. Something would have to cause some level of urgency. I went through a number of possibilities. Maybe the train has to deliver needed disaster relief supplies. The thing is, in the real world, who would refuse to help in a situation like that? In fact, everything else would stop and all efforts would goto assisting in whatever the disaster was. A crucial part of the story is that others turn down the request for help, leaving only the little engine left to get the job done. So what situation would create a degree of time sensitive urgency but not to the level where it would be unreasonable for others to refuse to help? The answer came by making it a Christmas story. Christmas gave the ideal set up for why the train had to make it that day but where it was also reasonable and understandable as to why others wouldn't step up to help.   The answer was perfect and it even allowed the train to keep the cargo of toys and food from the source material. From there, I was off, trading in anthropomorphic trains for human characters. Our heroine, Connie, is a short, petite female to reflect the original anthropomorphic little engine. Dutch is introduced so she has someone to converse with, allowing exposition and explanations of the problems and solutions before and during their journey over the mountain. Our two characters also complement each other. Connie is the plucky, spunky one who charges into action; Dutch is the pragmatic one who prefers to think things through first. Both are competent in their jobs at the controls of a train engine yet each has their different strengths.   Connie has the knowledge of the route and Dutch knows engine 12. They work together as a team and because of it, are able to accomplish their mission.

An important aspect I added that I feel builds on the story's original message: you have to give yourself a reason to believe you can do what it is you are trying to do. The underlying message from the original story is important. Being confident is the first step to success and never giving up will get you across the finish line. However, somewhere in there, you have to know what you're doing and you have to be prepared. Do your homework and study the problem. Develop a course of action and be competent in the tasks necessary to execute the plan. Practice, train, and get the necessary skills & experience. In our case here, Connie & Dutch already have the required skills, so a training sequence wasn't necessary for this story but coming up with a game plan was key. Lastly, be flexible and ready to adapt to unforeseen issues along the way. You never know when that switch will be in the wrong position.

Just in case one may have missed the significance of the engine numbers, 12 & 24 make the date of Christmas Eve. Obviously the little engine got the smaller number and being half of 24 made for a perfect allegory to being little.

This story doesn't occur in any particular time or place. The setting is somewhere in the American west, near and in the Rocky Mountains. It's a time where diesel electric engines exist but steam engines are still in use to some degree. There are no cell phones or internet here either. That's all the set up we need to get our train up from the city of Garrison on the front range to the town of O'Neill in the mountains.

One last thing, a source of inspiration and Christmas spirit, the late, great Paul O'Neill. Yes, the name of Connie's hometown and last stop is a nod to him. For those who don't know, Paul O'Neill was the founder of Trans-Siberian Orchestra. He was not only a world class musician, songwriter, and producer, he was a story teller. He told incredible stories in the form of rock operas, marrying visuals with his music in amazing stage shows. On top of all that, he wrote additional stories that could be found in the album inserts and show programs. He redefined what Christmas music can be with brilliant original songs and transformative covers of traditional pieces. I hope my retelling of *The Little Engine that Could* is as transformative as his work. I hope this story is good enough for you to read again and, when you do, try it with a Trans-Siberian Orchestra soundtrack playing along in your head to cheer on our pair of heroes and their little engine.